CIVIC PARTICIPATION
Working for Civil Rights

WOMEN'S SUFFRAGE MOVEMENT

Jill Keppeler

PowerKiDS press.
New York

Published in 2017 by The Rosen Publishing Group, Inc.
29 East 21st Street, New York, NY 10010

First Edition

Editor: Caitie McAneney
Book Design: Mickey Harmon

Photo Credits: Cover (image), pp. 5, 7, 13, 15, 21, 23, 25 Everett Historical/Shutterstock.com; cover, pp. 1, 3–32 (background) Milena_Bo/Shutterstock.com; p. 6 Print Collector/Contributor/Hulton Fine Art Collection/Getty Images; p. 9 (Truth) MPI/Stringer/Archive Photos/Getty Images; p. 9 (Mott) Time & Life Pictures/Contributor/The LIFE Picture Collection/Getty Images; pp. 9 (Stanton),11, 15, 17, 27 Bettmann/Contributor/Bettmann/Getty Images; p. 19 Buyenlarge/Contributor/Archive Photos/Getty Images; p. 29 NurPhoto/Getty Images.

Cataloging-in-Publication Data

Names: Keppeler, Jill.
Title: Women's suffrage movement / Jill Keppeler.
Description: New York : PowerKids Press, 2017. | Series: Civic participation: working for civil rights | Includes index.
Identifiers: ISBN 9781499426854 (pbk.) | ISBN 9781499428452 (library bound) | ISBN 9781499426861 (6 pack)
Subjects: LCSH: Women–Suffrage–United States–History–Juvenile literature.
Classification: LCC JK1896.K47 2017 | DDC 324.6'230973–dc23

Manufactured in the United States of America

CPSIA Compliance Information: Batch #BW17PK: For Further Information contact Rosen Publishing, New York, New York at 1-800-237-9932

CONTENTS

CREATED EQUAL

"We hold these truths to be self-evident, that all men are created equal. . . ." Those are some of the most famous words ever written in the history of the United States of America. However, author Thomas Jefferson left out something rather important—women.

This line from the Declaration of Independence set the stage for freedom for all Americans, but even after the American Revolution, it was clear that some people had more freedoms than others. The women of the United States had to fight for years to gain suffrage, or the right to vote in elections. These brave pioneers endured legal challenges, harsh criticism, and sometimes even physical **abuse**.

Today, thanks to the women's suffrage movement, all women in the United States have the right to vote. Women also hold some of the nation's highest political offices.

The women who fought for the right to vote in the United States were very brave. Many people thought they should not have this right, but they kept fighting.

SETTING THE STAGE

The fight for women's suffrage in the United States grew from a larger struggle for women's rights. In the early days of the United States, there were many **stereotypes** and expectations about women's place in society. Many people believed that women were only supposed to be involved in **domestic** concerns.

Mary Wollstonecraft

An Early Leader

Women in Great Britain began fighting for the right to vote around the same time the suffrage movement in the United States began. In 1792, a British woman named Mary Wollstonecraft published *A Vindication of the Rights of Women*. Wollstonecraft was one of the first to call for suffrage for women. She also said the educational systems of the time trained women to be helpless and that women and men should receive equal educations.

However, many American women began to reject the idea that their only true purpose was to be wives and mothers who were only concerned with the home. They were interested in being a real part of society and making a difference. In the 1800s, there were many **reform** groups whose members wanted to change society for the better. Many American women wanted to be involved—and to be taken seriously while they did so.

Many women who wanted the right to vote were wives and mothers. They wanted to be respected as people with minds and goals too.

ANOTHER FIGHT FOR FREEDOM

Some of the women who would lead the U.S. women's suffrage movement were first involved in the abolitionist movement, which sought to end slavery in the United States. However, some abolitionist groups didn't accept female members and the ones that did often kept women out of leadership **roles**. Sisters Angelina and Sarah Moore Grimké were criticized because they made speeches against slavery to groups that contained both men and women.

In 1840, abolitionists Lucretia Mott and Elizabeth Cady Stanton traveled to London, England, for the World Anti-Slavery Convention—but they and other women were forced to watch instead of actually taking part. Mott, Stanton, and many other women came to the conclusion that, to be taken seriously as reformers, they first needed the right to vote.

Before they fought for women's suffrage, these leaders of the women's suffrage movement fought to end slavery.

Sojourner Truth

Elizabeth Cady Stanton

Lucretia Mott

A Powerful Speaker

Sojourner Truth, born Isabella Baumfree, fought for both abolition and women's suffrage. She was born into slavery around 1797 in New York State and escaped in 1827. Truth joined the abolitionist movement in the 1840s and the women's suffrage movement in the 1850s. She may be best known for a speech she delivered in 1851. This speech, which came to be known as "Ain't I a Woman?", showed the struggle of being both black and a woman.

COMING TOGETHER

Many people mark the beginning of the U.S. women's suffrage movement as July 1848, when the first women's rights convention took place in Seneca Falls, New York. More than 200 people attended the event, which Lucretia Mott and Elizabeth Cady Stanton organized.

During the convention, Stanton read a Declaration of Sentiments that outlined the rights that women should have. It included the line "We hold these truths to be self-evident, that all men *and women* are created equal. . . ." Of those who attended, 100 people signed it, including 68 women and 32 men.

The convention also produced a dozen **resolutions**, one of which called for women's suffrage. The resolution concerning the right to vote was very **controversial**. Many thought it should be removed, but Stanton argued in its favor. The resolution stayed.

Elizabeth Cady Stanton and Women's Rights

In this illustration, Elizabeth Cady Stanton speaks at the 1848 women's rights convention. In 1998, Seneca Falls hosted a celebration marking the 150th anniversary of the convention. Hillary Clinton spoke at the event.

After the Seneca Falls convention, organizers started to plan many more women's rights conventions. The first National Women's Rights Convention took place in October 1850 in Worcester, Massachusetts. It was organized by Paulina Wright Davis and other suffragists, or people working for voting rights.

The event featured **debates**, speakers, and plans for the future of the movement. More than 1,000 people attended. While participants talked about many topics, suffrage was a main focus. For some time after this, national women's rights conventions were held every year.

However, just as the women's suffrage movement was really getting started, the U.S. Civil War began in 1861. Many who took part in the movement refocused their energy on helping the war effort.

Many men, including those who worked for magazines and newspapers, made fun of the women's rights movement. This print shows a scene mocking a women's rights convention in 1859.

In the Press

Some newspaper reporters who attended the convention criticized the event, those who attended it, and their goals. A reporter for the *New York Herald* wrote in horror that Abby Kelley, one of the speakers, "urged that the work should be **commenced** by educating both sexes together, and that all distinctions in society between man and woman should be abolished, and that a woman was just as well qualified to be President as a man."

SUSAN B. ANTHONY

One of the most famous fighters for U.S. women's suffrage was Susan B. Anthony, who was born in 1820 in Massachusetts. As a young woman, she worked as a teacher for about 10 years and became active in **temperance** and abolitionist groups. In 1851, she met Elizabeth Cady Stanton and the two began working together toward the cause of women's rights.

Anthony was a powerful writer and speaker. She worked with Stanton in publishing the *Revolution*, a newspaper in which they shared their views. Anthony traveled across the country speaking about women's rights. She had to **contend** with a great deal of criticism and abuse from people who didn't want to hear what she had to say. Still, Anthony worked toward suffrage right up until her death in 1906.

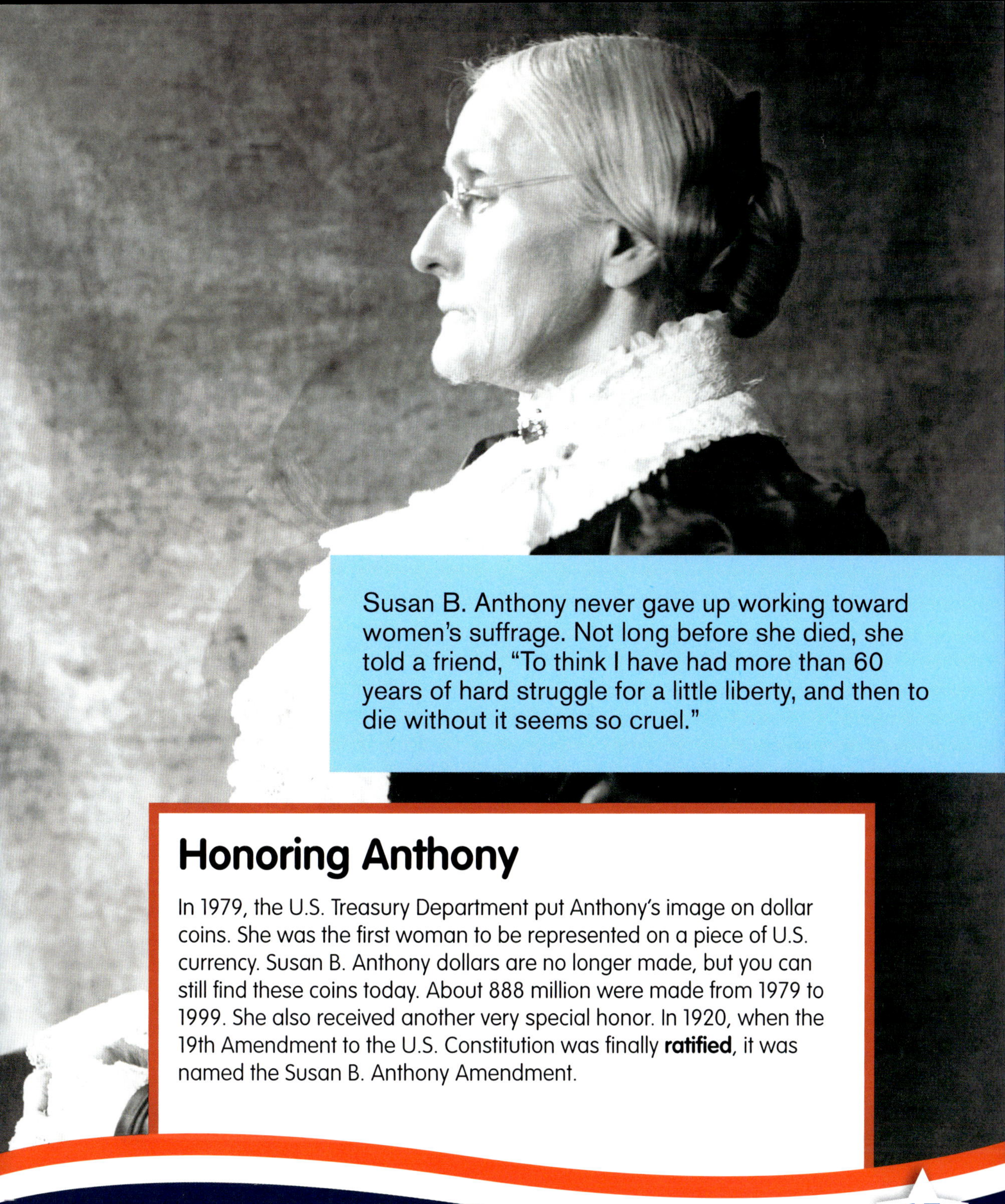

Susan B. Anthony never gave up working toward women's suffrage. Not long before she died, she told a friend, "To think I have had more than 60 years of hard struggle for a little liberty, and then to die without it seems so cruel."

Honoring Anthony

In 1979, the U.S. Treasury Department put Anthony's image on dollar coins. She was the first woman to be represented on a piece of U.S. currency. Susan B. Anthony dollars are no longer made, but you can still find these coins today. About 888 million were made from 1979 to 1999. She also received another very special honor. In 1920, when the 19th Amendment to the U.S. Constitution was finally **ratified**, it was named the Susan B. Anthony Amendment.

COMPETING GROUPS

After the Civil War ended in 1865, women were ready to get back to work for suffrage. In 1866, Elizabeth Cady Stanton and Susan B. Anthony started the American Equal Rights Association, which was dedicated to gaining voting rights for all.

Unfortunately, the organization soon ran into a problem. Many of those who fought for women's suffrage were against any amendment that gave former slaves the right to vote but did not give that right to women. Others thought that it was more important for African American men to earn the right first and that women could simply continue to fight.

In 1869, the American Equal Rights Association split over this issue. Stanton and Anthony formed the National Woman Suffrage Association. Other suffragists formed the American Woman Suffrage Association.

Lucy Stone was one of the founders of the American Woman Suffrage Association. She also served as its first president.

In 1870, the 15th Amendment to the U.S. Constitution gave African American men the right to vote. Despite their background as abolitionists, Elizabeth Cady Stanton, Susan B. Anthony, and others refused to work to get it ratified.

The members of the National Woman Suffrage Association, which was based in New York State, devoted themselves to working toward a women's suffrage amendment to the U.S. Constitution. The members of the American Woman Suffrage Association, which was based in Boston, Massachusetts, worked toward changing laws at the state level.

This split did not help their cause. Instead, it divided the supporters, their message, and the money they had available to work for it. In 1890, the two groups reunited, forming the National American Woman Suffrage Association. The cause began to gain ground again.

The offices of the National American Woman Suffrage Association are shown in Washington, D.C. Elizabeth Cady Stanton and Susan B. Anthony were the first two presidents of the group.

SMALL STEPS

Even though it was illegal, Susan B. Anthony and 15 other women voted in the U.S. election of 1872, during which President Ulysses S. Grant was running for re-election against Horace Greeley. Anthony voted for Grant and was arrested. She went to trial and fought the charges but was fined $100 ($1,887 in today's currency)—which she refused to pay.

In 1878, for the first time, members of the U.S. Congress discussed a proposed amendment for women's suffrage. And, in the meantime, a few states began to approve women's suffrage on their own. In 1890, the state of Wyoming was admitted to the Union with a state constitution that already gave women the right to vote. By 1900, Colorado, Utah, and Idaho had given women the right to vote as well.

In this image, Victoria Woodhull is shown addressing a congressional committee on women's suffrage in 1872.

The First Female Candidates

Even though women did not yet have the right to vote, a woman ran for the office of president in the 1872 election. The Equal Rights Party nominated Victoria Woodhull. No one is sure how many votes she received. Belva Lockwood ran for president in the 1884 and 1888 elections. She received more than 4,000 votes in 1884. Lockwood was also the first female lawyer to argue in front of the U.S. Supreme Court.

INTO THE 20TH CENTURY

Unfortunately, despite their victories, the early members of the women's suffrage movement were growing older. Lucretia Mott died in 1880, followed by Elizabeth Cady Stanton in 1902 and Susan B. Anthony in 1906. Sadly, they were never able to cast a legal vote in a U.S. election.

However, new women stepped up to lead the suffrage movement. Carrie Chapman Catt took over the National American Woman Suffrage Association in 1900. Alice Paul, an American woman who studied in England and helped with the suffrage campaign there, started the National Women's Party in 1913.

As new leaders continued the fight, more states approved suffrage rights for women. By 1918, 11 more states, including California and New York, had given women full voting rights.

Women in New York State won the right to vote in 1917. The three women shown are about to vote for the first time.

PICKETING AND PRISON

When Alice Paul returned to the United States and started the National Women's Party, she brought **tactics** used by the more **militant** women's suffrage movement in England. Members of the group picketed the White House, which means they marched and stood outside while carrying signs.

In June 1917, police started arresting women who were picketing. Some were sentenced to up to six months in prison. While there, they were treated very badly. On what has become known as the "Night of Terror" on November 15, 1917, guards beat about 30 women who were in prison in Occoquan, Virginia.

By January 1918, a court overturned all the women's sentences. The same month, President Woodrow Wilson declared his support for a women's suffrage amendment.

Suffragists knew they could be arrested, but they protested for the right to vote anyway. Catherine Flanagan (left) and Madeleine Watson (right) of the National Women's Party are shown as they picket the White House in 1917.

THE 19TH AMENDMENT

All the work by Stanton, Anthony, Catt, Paul, and countless other women and men was finally about to pay off. When World War I started in 1914, the women of the United States—including many suffragists—played a huge role in keeping the country going during the war effort. Much **opposition** to women's suffrage broke down after the war ended in 1918.

In May 1919, the U.S. House of Representatives approved a constitutional amendment granting women the right to vote. The Senate approved it in June. It took about a year for enough states to ratify it, but on August 26, 1920, the 19th Amendment became law. The amendment says that all citizens of the United States have the right to vote.

A group of suffragists celebrate the passage of the 19th Amendment. More than 26 million women throughout the United States now had the right to vote.

Sole Survivor

Of the 68 women who signed the Declaration of Sentiments at the 1848 women's rights convention in Seneca Falls, only one was still alive when the 19th Amendment was ratified. Unfortunately, Charlotte Woodward Pierce, 92, was ill on the day of the 1920 presidential election and unable to vote. "My heart is with all women who vote," she said in 1921. "They have gained it now, and they should not quarrel about the method of using it."

THE FUTURE

The 19th Amendment was the single largest expansion of voting rights in U.S. history. In the years after its ratification, many members of the women's suffrage movement worked to earn more rights for women. More women started running for public office.

Today, women serve in many levels of government, from local city councils and school boards to the U.S. Congress. There are female justices on the U.S. Supreme Court. And, in 2016, Hillary Clinton became the first woman to be nominated by a major political party for the office of president of the United States.

Many women and men worked very hard so that all citizens of the United States can vote for our leaders. It's very important to exercise this right!

In July 2016, Hillary Clinton, who served as the U.S. Secretary of State from 2009 to 2013, accepted the Democratic Party nomination for president of the United States.

TIMELINE OF THE WOMEN'S SUFFRAGE MOVEMENT

1840
Lucretia Mott and Elizabeth Cady Stanton travel to London, England, for the World Anti-Slavery Convention but are not allowed to take part.

July 1848
The first women's rights convention takes place in Seneca Falls, New York. A Declaration of Sentiments is signed by 68 women and 32 men.

October 1850
The first National Women's Rights Convention takes place in Worcester, Massachusetts.

1866
Elizabeth Cady Stanton and Susan B. Anthony start the American Equal Rights Association.

1869
The American Equal Rights Association splits. Suffragists form the National Woman Suffrage Association (NWSA) and the American Woman Suffrage Association (AWSA).

1872
Susan B. Anthony and 15 other women vote in the presidential election. Anthony is arrested and tried. Victoria Woodhull runs for the office of president of the United States.

1890
The NWSA and AWSA reunite to form the National American Woman Suffrage Association.

1913
Alice Paul starts the National Women's Party.

August 26, 1920
The 19th Amendment is ratified, giving U.S. women the right to vote.

2016
Hillary Clinton becomes the first woman to be nominated by a major political party for the office of president of the United States of America.

GLOSSARY

abuse: Treatment that is physically or verbally harmful.

commence: To start.

contend: To try hard to deal with something.

controversial: Likely to give rise to disagreement.

debate: An event during which two people discuss or argue about a topic, often in front of a group of people.

domestic: Having to do with the home or family.

militant: Using force to support a cause or beliefs.

opposition: The act of opposing something.

ratify: To formally approve.

reform: To change something into an improved form or condition.

resolution: A formal expression of intent or will voted by an official body or assembled group.

role: A part that someone has in a family, society, or other group.

stereotype: The act of unfairly believing that all people with a certain characteristic are the same.

tactic: An action that is planned and used to reach a certain goal.

temperance: Relating to the practice of drinking little or no alcohol.

INDEX

WEBSITES

Due to the changing nature of Internet links, PowerKids Press has developed an online list of websites related to the subject of this book. This site is updated regularly. Please use this link to access the list: www.powerkidslinks.com/civic/women